I0716341

ALSO BY MANUEL ARENAS

Book of Shadows: Grim Tales and Gothic Fancies

THE BURNING EMBER MISSION OF HELLDORADO

THE BURNING EMBER MISSION OF HELLDORADO

Manuel Arenas

Illustrations by
Mutartis Boswell

THE JACKANAPES PRESS

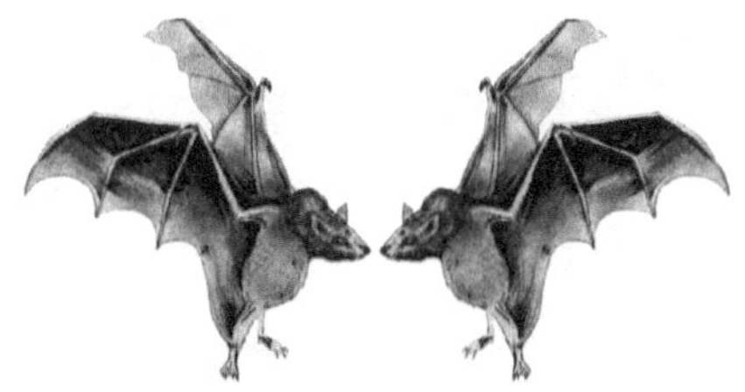

I would like to dedicate this collection to the folks at the now defunct Casanegra, a short-lived division of Panik House Entertainment, which specialized in films from the Golden Age of Mexican Horror. Films like *El Espejo de la bruja* (*The Witch's Mirror*, 1962) and *La maldición de la Llorona* (*The Curse of the Crying Woman*, 1963), with their admixture of European Gothic atmosphere and Mexican folkloric icons, really struck a chord with me that inspired the works featured in the pages you are about to read. Of course, I also wish to acknowledge the filmmakers and contributors to the original films, without whose inspired work none of this would have been possible.

Contents

SOUTHWESTERN GOTHIC

AN INTRODUCTION BY THE AUTHOR

IN THE FALL OF 2014, I came across a post on social media about a creature that would make the perfect pet for an aspiring Goth: a chicken that was entirely black. This was my introduction to the Ayam Cemani, a native fowl of Indonesia. I was so fascinated with this creature that I shared the post, joking that I needed to obtain one for a familiar. My friend Patricia Lynn Dompieri (author of the children's book *Lemon Bee and Other Peculiar Tales*) saw my share and challenged me to write a story about it. I accepted the challenge and spent the next few months trying to concoct a plot in which I could include the melanistic fowl. Embarrassed at how long it was taking me to come up with something, I wrote a quick haiku, on a lark, to show that I was actively working on it, and hadn't yet given up:

> *Ayam Cemani*
> *Finds a colonel in his feed:*
> *Tabuh Rah, black fowl.*

Eventually, I settled on a plot and after several revisions, ended up with a sprawling tale of colonialism, shapeshifting, and black magic, in the Sonoran

Desert. I believe this also may have been the first mention of Helldorado, my fictional city, *à la* Lovecraft's Arkham, where I base many of my Southwestern Gothic tales. Speaking of that haunted New England city, Arkham House founder August Derleth once penned a weird tale entitled *The Extra Passenger* that was adapted in 1961 for the seminal television anthology series *Thriller*, hosted by Boris Karloff, which appeared as a short segment in the episode *Trio for Terror*. In it, Simon, a young hood, decides to off his rich eccentric uncle Julian so he can cash in on his inheritance and use the money to lavish upon his demanding moll. Simon contrives an elaborate get-away plan, involving train timetables, which seems to go off without a hitch, but what he didn't count on was that Julian's familiar, a rooster, would not let this betrayal go unanswered. The adaptation is very effective, even where the original story was not, so I won't spoil the denouement by giving up any more details. Even so, I will say that the scene where Simon gets his comeuppance played through my mind on a loop when writing the scene where Zwartenberg confronts Mirruño and his band of scary men.

As with most of my stories, nothing is left to chance, and every detail has meaning, especially names. Mirruño is a bit of an in-joke, as *mirruña*, normally feminine, is Mexican slang for a little piece or morsel, whereas the gangster in my story is a mountain of a man. Although it is technically a corruption of the word, this would not be unheard of as it is filtered through the patois of second or third generation Chicanos. I use a lot of Spanish phrases in this story, mostly for local color, but anything of consequence is repeated in English. I have witnessed this in some of the Hispanic neighborhoods across the US (not just the Southwest) where people tend to use a lot of Spanglish, alternating words and phrases between

Spanish and English, or even repeating them for the benefit of those in the room who might not be able to follow one language or the other. Many times, the speaker is not fluent in either language and mistakes are made... and that is my excuse for anything I may have botched in translation while writing my story! Ha, ha, ha! (*¡Ja, ja, ja!)*

Like most of my earlier tales, "Burning Ember Mission" has a lot of dialog. I did this because I saw once in an interview with film director Roger Corman where he said that when adapting Poe and/or Lovecraft, the challenge is that the stories are usually brief and rely mostly on atmosphere, with little character development and barely any dialogue. I am not as enamored with Richard Matheson's adaptations of Poe's exquisite tales as many other seem to be, so I decided to preemptively sidestep the necessity for such ill-suited prattle being forced into the mouths of my characters and try my hand at writing my own dialogue. I leave it to you, dear reader, to be the judge of whether or not I was successful in that endeavor.

At 8,000 plus words, this epic tale is a hard sell to editors for inclusion in magazines, or even most short story anthologies. Therefore, I decided to create this bantam book, to get it out into the world. For the accompanying artwork I initially selected my good friend, Arizona artist Dick Kelly, who did such an incredible job on the Krampus chapbook I commissioned from him a few years back. Unfortunately, Dick had more important things on his plate to contend with and the project stalled. Eventually, I reluctantly decided to release him of his commitment and pass the project on to another friend, UK artist Mutartis Boswell, whose brilliant illustration and cover art work for Hippocampus Press, Jackanapes Press, and Mind's Eye Publications, has always impressed me. I feel that Mr. Boswell's penchant for the diabolic and the grotesque is perfect for this project, and the resultant illustrations speak for themselves.

"Zwartenberg the Necromancer" is a prose poem that I excised from an unfinished draft of the sequel to "Burning Ember Mission." I hope one day to complete the sequel, and include it along with any other Helldorado-related tales in a comprehensive collection.

Speaking of unfinished stories, sometimes when I get stuck writing a story and don't know how to proceed, I write a poem about a main character to better understand their motivations and solidify their attributes in my imagination. My piece of vampiric verse, "Thalía" (from *Spectral Realms* No. 9), is such a poem. A while back, I got stuck writing one of my Helldorado stories and decided to write about the main characters. I wrote a poem for the heroine, her anti-hero aunt, and the villain. The aunt's poem, "Lupe Scries the Mirror Black," found no takers upon submission, but my colleague Scott J. Couturier pleaded in its defense and insisted that I include it in this collection. "Altagracia's Lament," found its way into *Spectral Realms*, after a modicum of tweaking, but I could not find a market for "Dimas Akelarre." It has been suggested to me that the inclusion of various words and phrases in Spanish and Latin may put off some readers but I think nowadays anyone with an iPhone can pull up an online dictionary and look up any unfamiliar words if they care to. Thus, Dimas makes his doom-laden debut within these pages.

Back in the early aughts, I saw an episode of *Law & Order* which featured a woman who went around telling everyone that she was expecting but, in reality, she was suffering from the trauma of having a stillborn in her belly. Somehow, the carcass was never removed, due to a medical complication, which contributed to the perpetuation of her delusion. This story fascinated me to no end and the concept of a woman who carried the corpse of her stillborn baby inside of her stuck in the back of my mind, bubbling in the mire of my imagination for many years before I came up with the concept of Coffin-belly Mary, also known as Féretrina. I wrote the first draft around 2006, and have tinkered with it many times over the years. In May of 2014, I was invited to read at a local event called **Rise!** featuring poets and musicians in "A Night of Hispanic Poetry and Art." After a laudatory introduction by the emcee and event organizer, Deborah Montaño (née Berman), emphasizing the dark humor of what I customarily refer to as my "black-light verse," I presented them with this devastating fairy tale! Oddly enough, despite a few explicitly violent passages, it struck a chord with some of the female members in the audience, who sought me out afterward to tell me how they were moved by the story of Féretrina's trials and tribulations, as well as her eventual vindication. Despite this, Féretrina has met with rejection everywhere I have submitted it. It has been seen by some as nothing more than a revenge tale, but I see it as a mystical coming of age story, if you will. There is a revenge element, for sure, but there is so much more, as the protagonist is transformed from a street urchin into a folk hero, a champion of the oppressed, like a supernatural Billy Jack. As with "Gothilocks" before it, I tried to make the story into a series with Féretrina traveling around the Southwest, taking care of business using her newfound powers and communicating with the spirit of her son in the Underworld, but the project floundered and none of the subsequent stories packed the punch of the original tale, so I abandoned it. Local comic book artist Jesus "Jesse"

Gutierrez did a painting of Féretrina around this time, which came out a little curvier than I described her in the story, but it is still a compelling image.

I'll close with a **Trigger Warning**: there are things in these stories that may be upsetting to some people. There is colonialism, gang violence, murder, rape, racism, homophobia &c., but I assure you that I did not include them to be salacious or exploitative. I am, however, telling a horror tale, and I consider these things to be especially horrific.

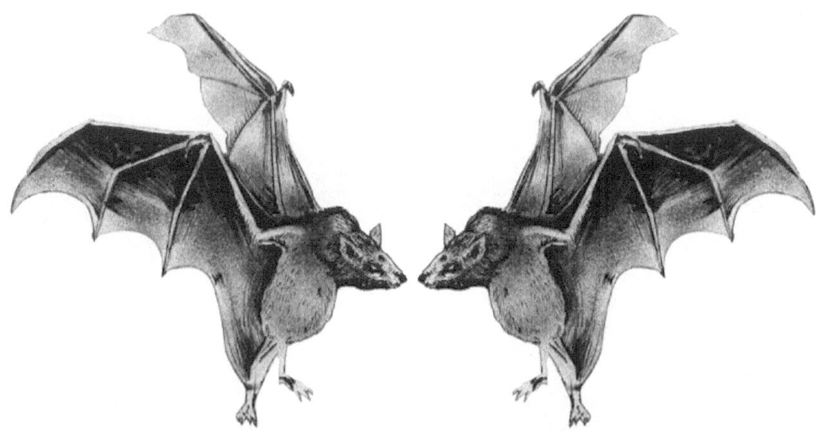

Helldorado

The Burning Ember Mission of Helldorado

I

ALTHOUGH SOME MIGHT HAVE it that Helldorado is just another name for Tombstone, Arizona, it is an actual place somewhere near Sedona. In fact, it is sort of the anti-Sedona, in the sense that it has a dark vortex which acts as a Hellmouth, spewing bleakness and doom into the desert. Invisible to regular folk, the sensitives say one can feel its black aura as an unsettling vibe when in its vicinity; beginning with a migraine headache, dizziness, horripilation of the flesh, then a roiling in one's gut, turning to nausea. Although the climate tends to a few degrees cooler than in the Valley, one must recall that, traditionally, not all of Hell is on fire. You won't find it on a map, nor would you find it driving unless you have business there, intentional or otherwise. It is a magnet for people of evil intent, and host to an array of unsavory characters ranging from small-time hoods to psychotic killers...and dark mages. This is truly a town where people dread sundown. Not all of the inhabitants of Helldorado are evil, though, and there are families and businesses who go on about their daily affairs like in most towns. Only, come nightfall, all of the good folk go to their homes and bar their doors against the things that come down from the mountains with the coyotes and mountain lions, prowling the shadows of night looking for sustenance and souls. A town like this, as one can imagine, holds many stories, and if its buff adobe walls could talk they would speak of horror and maleficia believed to have only existed in the long-ago past, if at all. One such story is the tale of Adrian Zwartenberg and the Burning Ember Mission.

Adrian is a tall, thin Dutchman with straw-colored hair, fading to gray. He is handsome in a professorial way, and dresses just a little young for his middle age. He speaks perfect English, albeit with a slight accent, and in casual conversation is prone to slip into a mixture of American and British idioms. He is polite, but cool, and generally keeps to himself, though he goes out and about enough (usually to the local watering hole, Cantina La Catrina, to prey on young debutantes) that townsfolk know who he is—and to avoid engaging him at all cost when they blunder into his path. He lives in a refurbished mission, which had once been the subject of much local lore. Apparently, it was built by a group of rogue Jesuit monks who separated from Padre Eusebio Kino, who was responsible for setting up missions throughout what was then known as *Pimería Alta* back in the late 17th and early 18th centuries, and is now part of southern Arizona in the United States as well as part of Sonora, Mexico. Drawn to the dark vortex, they set up camp in the area and, in the centuries since, the town of Helldorado grew around it.

As an affront to Kino and his Jesuit Order, the monks loosely modeled their unholy mission after the San Xavier del Bac mission in Tucson, Arizona, also known as "The White Dove of the Desert," but only superficially, and on a much smaller scale. Basically, they reproduced the structure of the chapel and added an underground catacomb for their library of black grimoires and, of course, quarters for the iniquitous monks. Although they never had the resources to completely reproduce the lavishness of the Tucson Mission, they made sure that wherever there was a religious figure or symbol in a relief on the façade of the original building, there was a gargoyle or blasphemous scene in the corresponding place on their mission. Crucifixes were turned on their heads, and nightmarish murals of Dantean diabolism covered its chapel walls, where satanic black masses were held in a mockery of Christian ritual. Since they employed the local sandstone in the fashioning of their mud bricks, the adobe structure bore a reddish hue, which made it look like a glowing coal thrown up from the Hellmouth, giving the ill-disposed mission its sobriquet. At a distance it blended in with the surrounding landscape, providing a small degree of obscurity. The satanic emissaries managed to dazzle a few natives from the Papago tribe (a name given to them by the Spanish; they are now recognized as the Tohono O'odham Nation) with their bacchanals and black masses, which differed so diametrically from the subdued rituals of their own people, securing their servitude with promises of unearthly pleasures and forbidden knowledge.

Although they practiced their blasphemy unchallenged in relative obscurity and impunity for over a century, they were finally shut down in 1820 by a final gasp of the Spanish Inquisition before the region was relinquished to the Mexicans the following year. The monks somehow contrived to protract their lifespans an unnaturally long time, yet without showing a day of wear on their wicked brows since their exile from the Society of Jesus; this way, when the Devil finally came to claim their souls they would still bear the fresh faces of the impetuous youths they had been when they first pledged him their troth. Their collection of grimoires and forbidden tomes was never found by the Inquisition: apparently, they took inspiration from the offshoot of the razed Library of Alexandria at the Serapeum and hid their black library underground, making it a truly *occult* library.

Despite the onslaught of the enforcers of the Holy Office much of the mission's structure remained intact save for some dashed idols and a cracked window or two, though the murals were whitewashed to blot their blasphemy. The inhabitants, however, did not fare as well. The ones who weren't killed in the initial skirmish were dragged out into the courtyard, where they were swiftly tried and burned in an auto-da-fé. Once the deed was done the Holy Inquisition left the area, the structure to be repaired and maintained by the few acolytes who had survived by hiding in the mission churchyard. After the dust had settled, they emerged to salvage what they could, but were wary of what might still be lurking in the halls of the mission after sunset.

So they built their own makeshift quarters out of earth, ocotillo branches, and saguaro ribs, where they drank cactus wine and tried to ignore the faint-but-grim chanting issuing from the chapel, as well as the sound of muted voices and shuffling footsteps which seeped in through the cracks of the structure during the night while they awaited the dispelling dawn. Despite their apparent misgivings, they kept the grounds and guarded the graves of their mentors, but lacked the swart conviction of their former masters for continuing their blasphemies. In the latter part of the 19th century the Anglo-American settlers began to flood in, bringing with them a new breed of "Christian soldiers," who laid siege to the mission. Its remaining inhabitants were run out of town, after which the structure fell into disrepair and neglect under the indifferent care of the local government. Even so, the vortex held sway in the end, and the second attempt to topple this beacon of darkness in the desert was quelled.

***

Enter Adrian Zwartenberg, who came to the mission on a black pilgrimage in the early aughts of the 21st century. He was so taken with the mission and the isolation of the area that he purchased and restored the building to its original satanic glory. He converted the monk's quarters into his home, and added modern amenities; he had the stained-glass windows repaired, the murals restored, and the termite-ridden balconies replaced with Makassar Ebony from Indonesia, which he made a special trip to purchase. Although he had not been officially employed by any specific entity for several decades, Zwartenberg somehow managed to accumulate much wealth over the years, which he kept in Swiss accounts. Despite his wealth, however, he dressed poorly and always in black, usually in mismatched shades of the color. He sometimes took his meals at local eateries, where he always paid in cash; generally, he showed no other outward sign of his affluence aside from his elaborate home, his black 1961 Jaguar E-Type sports car, and his regular trips to far-flung places of the world for his "research."

I say "research," quote-unquote, because everyone knows that he abandoned his profession of religious anthropologist years ago. It is whispered that Zwartenberg is now into some strain of dark magic, which he latched onto as a young man during his travels in the UK to study the origins of the mid-20th century resurgence of the old religions and the practice of witchcraft following the 1951 repeal of the Witchcraft Act of 1736. It is rumored that he studied the black arts at a fabled satanic school in the Transylvanian region of Romania, and at one point had ties to a particular university of metaphysics somewhere in New England until they banned him for inappropriate use of materials from the rare book room at the campus' extensive occult library.

Not long after settling in Helldorado, he seemed to fall under the spell of a Mexican-American shaman named Diego, a slight, short, but impishly handsome fellow replete with an aigrette of coarse, pomade-slickened black hair, which he combed away from his narrow forehead like a cresting wave so as not to obstruct his lively brown eyes and broad, friendly smile which he used to charm his marks. Diego claimed to be a *nahual* or shapeshifter, among other things, which Adrian had a marked interest in learning about. The two became unlikely fast friends, and Diego soon took up residence in Zwartenberg's house for the better part of a year.

At first folks in town thought the shaman, who was notorious for hoodwinking starry-eyed New Age tourists in Sedona into giving him wads of cash to teach them the secrets of the indigenous tribes of the Southwest *à la* Carlos Castañeda, had taken advantage of Zwartenberg. That is, until Diego started showing up at the local watering hole, Cantina La Catrina, red-eyed and disheveled, to get tanked and shoot off his mouth about Zwartenberg's unsavory proclivities and his collection of black grimoires. Apparently, one night, as he sat quaffing tall shots and blabbing, his glass exploded just inches away from his twiggy brown fingers as they reached for another swig. Startled, the man turned around sharply, his handsome, suntanned features distorting into a mask of dread as he yelped at the sight of Zwartenberg emerging from the shadows in the back of the room. He spun round on his stool and leapt off at a sprint into the night, but Adrian just ambled toward the bar, smiling like a house cat that swallowed a pet canary, casually sauntering out of the cantina door in the direction of his lair. That was the last most folks saw of Diego for some time.

Not long after, Zwartenberg fell afoul of a small-time dope dealer named Mirruño (an ironic nickname which is a play on the Mexican term *mirruña*, which means "tiny," the diametrical opposite of the hulk that he was), when he shamelessly propositioned his moll, Orfalinda, a dark-eyed beauty with lush black hair, skin the color of burnt umber, and curves more treacherous than a winding mountain road. She categorically rebuffed him, which did not sit well with the dissolute Dutchman. Still, determined to have his way, he tried to entice her with promises of riches and unimaginable pleasures, to which the feisty beauty riposted, *"¡Ni en este mundo, ni la otra, viejo verde; no quiero nada de ti!"* (essentially, "Neither in this life nor the other, dirty old man; I want nothing from you!").

In retaliation for Orfalinda's spurning of his advances, Zwartenberg left a ligature and a jar underneath Mirruño's RV, both of which contained unsavory charms intended to bring discord to their intimacy. Mirruño was a jealous type, and did not appreciate the insult to his *hyna* nor the bad mojo, so he paid Adrian a visit with a few of his more menacing *vatos*. When no one answered the door, they trashed the man's vintage car, which had been left parked outside with a car cover to protect it from the sun's blanching rays. However, the ruffians found that no matter how they tried, they could not gain entrance into the chapel nor the house proper. Expecting retaliation and spoiling for a fight, Mirruño put out the word that if that *joto holandés* had any real *cojones* he would face him directly, *como un hombre verdadero*, and "take what's coming to him instead of hiding in his house behind locked doors like a chickenshit." In his further harangues, of which there were many, he would frequently revert to the chicken analogy in his references to the Dutchman, but Zwartenberg never responded, and furthermore was not seen in town for many months afterward. Eventually, Mirruño let it go, and word spread around that Zwartenberg had skipped town to avoid a drubbing from the drug dealer and his band of scary men. Thus he was labeled a poltroon and derided as a "chicken"—again.

One evening, as Mirruño and his vatos were swilling bottles of cerveza and trading tall tales of their exploits, Diego, whom no one had seen in town for several months, strolled into Cantina La Catrina and sat down at the bar for his customary tequila shots. There was, however, something different about his carriage; he was a changed man. He was quieter, sullen, and haggard-looking. Gone was the exuberance and charm he once exuded. His brown eyes stared out from his now crow-footed eyelids like dark amber orbs with inclusions of death's-heads that cast a pall over everything they rested their bloodshot, stolid gaze upon.

He sat, solemnly, in a livery of white with a red kerchief tied (just so) about his throat, looking very much like a paradoxical mashup of peladito and señorito, and drank his shots in silence. Not believing his eyes, Mirruño slowly rose from his bar-stool and approached Diego. He looked him over with protuberant eyeballs, fit to burst with pique, then nodding his head sharply, tapped Diego on the shoulder with enough force to spill his drink. At this Diego just turned, unfazed, and smiled. Mirruño sneered at the trickster. "*Oye, Cantinflas, donde está el gabacho con quien andavas?* Where is that white guy you used to hang out with?"

Diego replied calmly, "Ba'al Zwartenberg is out of town on business, but he will be back soon enough."

"Bahl? *Boludo* is more like it!" Mirruño retorted.

Diego replied in a calm and cautious tone, as if speaking to a child who doesn't know well enough to let sleeping dogs lie, "*Ba'al* is an honorific title meaning lord, or Master. Because you really have no idea who you are trying to provoke, I will give you this friendly word of warning. I am a fraud, I think you all know that by now," here he cast a brief glance at Mirruño's crew, who sat expectantly at their table, hands by their respective sides. "I can say that with no amount of guilt because I have already paid for my sins tenfold. Once he sussed me out as a phony, Ba'al Zwartenberg blackmailed me into being his footman—his servant, if you will. He threatened to expose me as a fraud, ruin my reputation and my livelihood. It was then I was conscripted into his dark ranks. Since I couldn't really teach him the shape-shifting ways of a *nahual,* he found out what he needed to know on his own using the books in his library. After your last visit to the house, we spent many months traveling around the world. He has taken me to places I never dreamed of seeing, shown me things I may never dream again without seeing. If I may say so, my friend, I think it best for you to lay low and be glad the devil has his focus on other things for now."

"*Me vale madres* what you think, *chavalo*! You tell that *viejo verde* that I am going to make him wish he never laid his squinty pervert eyes on my Orfalinda next time we meet!" Seething with his machismo, he snatched Diego's freshly refilled drink from his hand and swallowed it in a loud gulp before slamming the empty glass on the bar counter. Looking at the resigning man, he winked, took a few quick breaths, passed his large olive-skinned hand over his bald pate, then turned to shoot a sharp glance at his men, who all stood to attention. At a firm nod from their boss, they followed him out of the cantina.

***

A week had passed since the cantina confrontation when a renovated Jaguar S1 was seen to crawl up the winding driveway leading to Zwartenberg's lair in the small hours of the night with its headlights turned off. Mirruño, however, had men watching the house, so he was soon apprised of what appeared to be Zwartenberg's much-anticipated return, though the driver was never actually seen to alight from the car, which pulled into the garage (a recent add-on), the door of which closed quickly behind it. Not surprisingly, the Dutchman failed to make any confirmatory public appearance at any time thereafter.

Then the nightmares came. Orfalinda began to have *pesadillas*, nightmares, about a *gallo infernal* that would strut about the foot of her bed; a big black rooster, the size of a human child, clawing at the carpeted floor, with its left wing stretched downward, walking widdershins while a paralyzing dark cloud pressed upon her chest and distant voices droned a darksome chant. These went on for almost a fortnight before the dream became a horrific reality.

Orfalinda's torment reached its crescendo when she was awakened by an unearthly rooster crow. Confused, she turned her groggy head to see the time on her digital clock read 13:00. Not registering the hour, she nevertheless sensed somewhere in her sleep-addled brain that something was amiss. A surge of gooseflesh rippled over her naked body as she then heard the sinister chanting from her dreams with her conscious ears. Hesitantly, she looked to the foot of her bed and saw the black rooster, blacker than the shadows of the lightless room, oppressing her with its stultifying gaze as it grew in height and girth, like an inflating balloon figure, until it popped with a burst of static electricity into a cloud of black dust particles which hovered in the air, swirling over her bed. Somewhere in the darkness an unseen hand drew down her bedclothes, revealing her bare supine form.

Panicking, Orfalinda turned to rouse Mirruño, calling him by his true name, Marcelo, but no matter how much she shook, prodded, punched, or screamed at her bedfellow, he would not respond. Looking to his nightstand, she recoiled at the gruesome sight of a severed hand, coated in a greasy substance and tipped with flaming wicks, upon the palm of which was carved a lidless eye. Gradually, she found that her limbs were becoming numb and weighty, and soon she was paralyzed as the swirling mass above her transmogrified into an icy black brume that engulfed her in its sooty tendrils. Somehow, this intangible entity commenced to assault her physically as she tried to scream through her frozen throat.

In confirmation of her harrowing ordeal, Orfalinda awoke the next day to find her person covered in the tell-tale signs of the brutal and involuntary coition. Mirruño, awakened by the sobs of his ladylove, was beside himself. Trying very hard to contain his anger and horror, he did his best to calm Orfalinda down enough to hear her tale of the previous night's visit from the gallinaceous incubus and the paralyzing power of the now-absent *main de gloire*.

Because of her questionable status as a citizen, Orfalinda could not retain a regular doctor, so she went to the Helldorado Free Clinic, where she could get some basic care with few questions asked. In the waiting room she kept having flashbacks of her hellish night every time the lids of her sleep-deprived eyes endeavored to close and afford her some respite. Although she spoke little English, there was a translator on hand who accompanied her into the examination room once she was called upon to be seen by a volunteer medical student. The young woman quickly surmised that her patient had been the victim of a sexual assault and bid the translator ask if Orfalinda wanted to speak to someone about reporting what had happened to her, but Orfalinda just began to hyperventilate, tears running in hot salty streams down her flushed cheeks.

The women did their best to assure her she was in a safe environment and could speak freely without fear of exposure or reprisal. They asked her if she knew her assailant personally, and whether it was her companion in the waiting room, to which Orfalinda emphatically responded in the negative.

"No, no!" she shouted. "*No fue Marcelo, fue un gallo infernal—un demonio!*"

A demon! An infernal rooster, no less? Preposterous! thought the interpreter, who was convinced the young woman was either covering for someone or, worse, had lost her senses due to the trauma of what she had experienced. Even so, she translated Orfalinda's account of the events faithfully, albeit with a modicum of scorn. After the implementation of the SAFE kit, the doctor hugged Orfalinda and gave her a business card, as well as the card of an advocate in case she changed her mind about reporting the assault.

Mirruño, beside himself with grief and anger, was now on the war path. He told his man Chuy to let him know as soon as there was any sign of anyone leaving the enchanted mission. Chuy sent an enthusiastic young thug named Javi to keep an eye on the place, and to take pictures of the layout for an imminent assault. When he did not check in the next day Chuy sent Alejo, one of Mirruño's bodyguards, to the lookout post just outside the mission walls. There, Javi's body was found in the driver's seat of a parked (not-so-inconspicuous) Chevy Impala convertible, top up, with his eyes gouged out. In the passenger seat to his right lay a camera with a cracked long-range lens that looked crunched, like a discarded soda can. Needless to say, the memory card had been extracted. Not eager to lose any more men, Chuy arranged to have a small drone sent out to scout the area periodically. The following evening, Mirruño got his wish when Diego was seen to leave the mission and go to the Cafe La Calaca, an adjunct to Cantina La Catrina, which served coffee, pastries, and a Mexican lunch menu.

When Mirruño arrived, Diego looked hungover, hovering over a bowl of *pozole* and desperately grasping a tall glass of *Agua Fresca de Jamaica* (cold hibiscus tea). Slowly inhaling the aroma of the spicy broth beneath an indoor mural reproduction of the Posada print bearing the image of the establishment's namesake, lost in reverie, Diego mused over how the cooked hominy kernels looked like little skulls floating in a cauldron of sacrificial flesh. Much like the ritual stew of his ancestors in pre-Columbian times...he wondered whether the stewed flesh of his enemies would taste anything like the pork chunks in his bowl.

As if on cue, Mirruño burst into the cafe like a bull barreling down on a red flag, but Chuy grabbed his boss' arm before he did something he would later regret.

"Where is he? Where is that *hijo de puta* Zwartenberg? Tell me now so I can go kill him, or else I will kill you first!"

Turning to look at the brute who towered over his table, Diego raised his hand in a halting manner and calmly replied, "*Cuidado amigo*, we are in a public place, where open threats like that can land a man in a cot at the Helldorado hoosegow. What has gotten you so upset this time?"

"I'll tell you what, that *ruco* sent some devil chicken to my house and it made my girlfriend pregnant!"

"Wait...what? A *devil chicken*? So, does that make you a cluckold now?" Diego snickered, barely able to contain his amusement at his own quip.

This set the larger man off. Mirruño grabbed Diego by his shirt collar and landed a punch on his mouth, which knocked him to the ground.

"You think you're funny, *chavolo*? We'll see if your tongue still says funny things when you're wearing it as a necktie!"

"*¡Oye, ustedes dos no se pueden pelear aquí!*" shouted the woman behind the counter, "Take your fight outside!"

Mirruño, either not hearing or caring what the proprietor of the cafe said, reared back for a second blow, but Diego put out his hand again and shouted:

"Wait! Wait...you said you think a chicken is responsible for your girlfriend's attack? Okay, let's say that were possible. Ba'al Zwartenberg does have a black chicken named Magistellus that he keeps as a familiar, which he picked up during his trip to Indonesia to buy some special wood for the mission renovations. Let's say I can get you access to this bird, what would you do then?"

"What would I do? I'd kill it and make *pollo frito* with it, then make that smug bastard eat it before I killed him too!"

"I have a better idea, *amigo mio*. What if we kidnap the bird? I've read some of the old books in Zwartenberg's occult library, and there was one that spoke of a black chicken that could literally lay golden eggs!"

"Golden eggs? *No mames güey*, that's a fairytale. What, you think I'm some kind of *pendejo* or something?"

Here Diego smiled. Even through split lips and blood-stained teeth, the charming grin that opened the purse strings of lonely dowagers—and the legs of pretty ingénues—appeared on his boyish face. Using the leg of his table for support, Diego rose from the café floor and, with the confidence of a grifter, threw his left arm around the broad shoulders of his burly attacker, who quickly tensed up. Diego ignored this and spoke softly, in a conspiratorial fashion.

"Quite the opposite, Mr. Mirruño. I see you rather as a smart man, who knows a good thing when he hears it. You question the veracity of my claim, which is understandable, but have you ever known Ba'al Zwartenberg to work a regular job? Where does all his wealth come from then, eh? How do you think he pays for all his trips? Perhaps this familiar is his source of wealth. *Mira*, I'm tired of being under the yoke of this *güero*, and would like to teach him a lesson too. But I would also like to get something to make up for all the time I've lost being under his thumb, and this golden goose—I mean chicken—could be just the payoff we both want. The best time to take the brujo by surprise is when he is practicing his devotions...at dusk."

II

In the ensuing days Diego plotted with Mirruño to overthrow his coercive Master. In the meantime, a very distraught Orfalinda contacted the young doctor at the clinic, screaming in Spanish and in sporadic, broken English that she was carrying the devil's child and needed an abortion. The doctors at the clinic agreed to have her come in with the intent of doing a prenatal exam and to persuade her of other options; however, upon arrival she was found to already be heavy with child. After an examination and an ultrasound, it was determined that, miraculously, she was indeed in an advanced state of pregnancy—too advanced to perform an abortion. Although they could see something in the ultrasound image, a form misshapen and non-human, they could not access it, nor breach her pudenda to do anything about it. Over the next few weeks, as her abdomen swelled so her sanity slipped, until one ill-starred evening she simultaneously "gave light" as her spirit went towards the light in the infirmary at the St. Simeon Psychiatric Hospital. Orfalinda, in a paroxysm of terror, shrieked her last breath at the sight of her chimerical cherub as it clawed and slithered its way from her womb, mauling the venerable doctor and the attendant nurse with its infant claws. The *lusus naturae* raged through the hospital halls, terrorizing patients and staff, until it discovered its leathery wings, which it unfurled as it crashed through an office window and flew into the hot desert night.

If there were ever any lingering doubts in the minds of his henchmen as to his determination to do so, Mirruño assured his men that they were going to kill Zwartenberg. And, once they had what they wanted from Diego, the sorcerer's lackey was to be dispatched as well.

III

Mirruño and his gang parked their cars at the bottom of the pathway leading up to the lair of the sorcerer, then proceeded to walk up the winding trail until the mission-house came into view as a silhouette against the darkening sky. A reddened moon was just materializing in the gloaming, giving it a foreboding aspect, but these men were fueled with self-righteous anger and adrenaline and would not be deterred from their bloody purpose. The plan was to go into the house and dispose of Zwartenberg in the most prejudicial manner they could muster, then see Diego about this gold-laying chicken.

So as not to be conspicuous, they walked off the path through the teddy-bear cholla, with their prickly "jumping" spurs that catch in one's clothes when brushed against. This resulted in a few muffled expletives from the men, who had foolishly stormed through the brush without being mindful of the flora, but for the most part they reached the house without incident, save for a growing nausea which seeped into the core of their stomachs when they first stepped upon the trail and worsened the further they advanced into the compound. Approaching the side gate, they found it unlocked and cautiously slipped in under the cover of dusk, staying close to the walls. As the encroaching shadows of twilight engulfed the purposeful party, the vesperal lull was shattered by an unearthly cockcrow, which gave the men a momentary pause as they stared into one another's faces.

Mirruño's man Chuy was selected to be the one to nick the golden fowl (and dispose of Diego once it was procured). Breaking from the original raiding party, which stayed behind to enter the chapel, he skulked to the rear of the mission, down a pathway lined on either side with panels depicting a panoply of skeletons, cavorting in a danse macabre, which led to the mortuary chapel. On the side of the chapel, behind a fence of tall, spiny ocotillos, rose thirteen headstones, one for each of the original founding friars of the mission. Upon every sun-blanched marker was graven an inverted pentagram. The tiny red flowers at the tips of the ocotillo stalks looked like little flames. Glancing to his left, Chuy was startled by what he initially thought were two people lurking in the shadows. It turned out to be a tableau, a life-size diorama, replicating the initial appearance of Mephistopheles to Faust, apparently another of Zwartenberg's renovation add-ons. Shaking his head and cursing himself under his breath for being spooked so easily, he continued down the thorny path to the red adobe chapel. As he approached the doorway, he was met by a surprisingly chipper Diego.

"Hey bro, you made it!"

"Shush! Keep it down, dude. You don't want to give us away, do you?" chided Chuy.

"Huh? Oh yeah...I mean no, right...right you are!" replied Diego in a conspicuously loud whisper. Then, motioning for Chuy to follow, he led him to the chapel door, an ebony portal which curiously bore no metal, only a heavy wooden bolt which was locked. Looming over the entrance from a transom window were actual skull-and-crossbones set onto red stained glass. Diego muttered an unintelligible incantation over the lock, and the bolt shot open.

Smiling, he turned and, with a wink, said to Chuy, "A handy trick I learned from the Master!"

Once inside, it was so dark Chuy could not see an inch away from his face. The stifling air was a miasma of incense, expired candle smoke, and another not-quite-definable odor, the identification of which Chuy was not too eager to know. His heart began racing with apprehension.

Mercifully, the familiar scraping sound of a match strike was followed by a spark of flame which, although small, helped to dispel his growing panic. Chuy's eyes followed the little flame as it sought out a flambeau in a sconce wrought into the semblance of a coiling snake, which consequently erupted into a flurry of warmth and light. Again, he saw that the now-illumined face of Diego bore that unsettling smile of his. Was this the same mask he wore for his marks at the Sedona thoroughfare?

Turning to the room, Chuy recoiled when he spied a glass casket containing a recumbent mummified corpse, a jade amulet strung about its desiccated neck. The body rested on a crimson catafalque behind an altar covered with expended varicolored votive candles: single melted stubs of gold, green, and purple alongside several of brown, red, and black. In the foreground was a black bowl filled with the charred remains of some offal that Chuy hoped came from an animal. Diego walked to the far corner of the shadowed room and lit a tall candelabra, which illuminated a shrine featuring an inverted crucifix with a very nonplussed-looking Christ on it. Behind that was a black-robed figure of the Santa Muerte, with her hands outstretched, in which she held a globe and a scythe respectively. About her waist was a knotted cord which bore an hourglass and a small scale. Chuy stared into her eyeless grinning skull-face and felt a chill ripple through his frame.

Trying not to show his fear, Chuy turned to Diego and quipped, "You know, there have been great advancements in electrical wiring since the time this place was originally built. You guys ever think of putting a few light switches in here? Could save a bundle on candle sticks and matches.”

“Aha! Good one!” Diego replied derisively. “No…the Master doesn’t wish to interfere with the structure or the vibrations of these ancient edifices. Though there is electricity in the main house.”

“Why do you call him ‘master?’” Chuy said through a sneer. “Are you his slave, or something? His bottom bitch?”

“No, I am not!” Diego snapped back. Anger flashed across his brow, quickly dissipating as he turned to light another candle, which revealed another shrine. This time the celebrated figure was a demon of some sort, with the torso of a man, a single rooster’s leg, and a dragon’s tail. On his shoulders he bore three heads: one of a man, which spat fire; one of a bull; and the last, a ram with curling horns. Due to his gallinaceous appendage, he was supported by two crutches.

“What the hell is that?!”

“That is ‘the Devil on Two Sticks,’ Asmodeus, one of the Seven Princes of Hell, and the demon of lust and vengeance! He walks with crutches because his foot is all cocked up, though sometimes he rides a lion with dragon wings.”

“You believe all of this hocus-pocus devil crap?” Chuy asked incredulously, but Diego only smiled again.

“Come on,” the grinning man countered, “let’s go meet our fowl friend. Oh yeah, and you should take a step back right about now.”

Walking to the inverted crucifix, Diego gingerly pulled on the top (or bottom, depending on one’s point of view) like a beer tap, which triggered a trap door in the floor in the very center of the room. However, the bouquet of the draft which issued from within was far from palatable.

"You want me to grab the torch?" Chuy asked, with an equal mixture of unease and disdain.

"No, there are some candlesticks by the bottom of the stairs we can light as soon as we descend."

As Diego went down the long stone staircase into the dark and musty catacomb, Chuy took one last look at the altars, crossing himself before following behind. In the shadows underneath the main altar, near a cooling puddle of candle wax, a bark scorpion cornered a cricket.

Once they touched cold clammy ground, Diego lit a flambeau, illuminating the cavernous room. Chuy marveled at its length, which must have stretched well beyond the dimensions of the aboveground chapel. Its high stone walls were covered in ebony bookshelves, each row over-stacked with crumbling ancient tomes. A tall ebon ladder leaned toward the shelves, attached to a trellis that spanned the uppermost part of the library. In a corner was a niche containing a rack holding brittle yellowed scrolls and large portfolio folders.

The room itself bore little furniture, save for a great ebon desk of intricate design, with what looked like a stylized bird talon at the end of the front left leg. Its companion to the right was a human foot, and the back legs were normal, albeit intricately carved, table legs. The desktop ended in a beveled trim with carven scales, and on the front of the desk was hewn another likeness of the demon Asmodeus, with his three heads. Behind the desk was an ebon chair with a plush red satin seat, a companion piece to the desk, upon which lay a small black book with a red ribbon bookmark keeping place in its pages. Diego sat in the chair, looked at Chuy, and nonchalantly pointed his finger in the direction of the bookshelves. "At the end of the shelves is a door with a judas window in the center," he said. "That is where you'll find the bird. You can go inside; it's unlocked at present."

Chuy, hesitant at first, walked down to the end of the bookshelves. As he passed the books he tried to see if he could recognize individual titles, but was not close enough to decipher the faded print on their withered spines. "How do you guys keep these old books from just turning to dust down here?" he asked, more as a distraction than out of real curiosity.

Catching the inflection of fear in his words, Diego responded, "Oh, you know, we use some 'Hints from Heloise' and a little domestic magic."

Realizing that Diego was not going to play along, he asked no more questions and continued walking down the lengthy hall, his footsteps sounding echo-less and flat on the stony walls. Reaching the end, he cautiously opened the door to what turned out to be a lightless cell. Peering inside, Chuy called out to Diego, "Dude, I can't see shit in here. Bring me a lantern or something, will you?"

"Sure thing!" responded Diego.

Appearing with a lantern in one hand and the small black book in the other, Diego handed the lamp to Chuy, then turned to the bookmarked page and made a show of reading something of great interest as he leaned on the jamb in the doorway.

Raising the lantern, Chuy inspected the contents of the cell.

"Man, there ain't nothing down here but some straw and a big black stone!" Chuy yelled angrily over his shoulder at Diego.

"That's no stone, that's an egg," Diego replied. Without lifting his eyes from the page, he slammed the cell door shut, the bolt of which automatically shot closed at his command. Opening the judas window in the middle of the door, Diego continued, "And what an egg it is, eh? Oh, we tweaked it a bit; said some chants over it, spilled some blood on it, and, voila, big black scary monster egg! Fascinating stuff, this Black Pullet—this is the grimoire I told you of. Well, not you specifically, your boss—but you were there! This is the one with the story about the black chicken that lays the golden eggs, but you know, I'm not so sure now that I got it right. You see, in this book it's a black 'pullet,' which is a young hen, that lays the golden egg, but Ba'al Zwartenberg's bird, Magistellus, well he's a rooster. Nevertheless, I do know another story about rooster eggs. In English lore it's said they hatch into a cockatrice, a hybrid dragon of sorts, half-rooster and half-serpent, which supposedly can kill a man with its gaze. Do you think that's what we have here in this egg? Shall we wait and see?"

With a few quick words from Diego, the lantern in Chuy's hand went dark. His betrayer then slammed the door shut and taunted, "Word to the wise: I reckon whatever is inside that egg is going to be hungry when it hatches." Unseen in the darkness, the color drained from Chuy's face, his bladder releasing a warm rivulet down his trouser leg when he heard the crackling sound of a monstrous beak pecking its way through the flat black surface of the over-sized ovum. Its unearthly squawk would be the last sound he ever consciously heard.

IV

Although spooked a bit by the eerie sound they'd just heard, Mirruño and his men walked slowly but with dread purpose to the chapel door, as per Diego's instructions. True to his word, they found it unlocked, and walked across the threshold single file into an embassy of Hell on Earth. The room was very dark, lit only by a grand candelabra behind the altar, with six candles in descending order on either side of a larger central taper. Mirruño mused on how it reminded him of a hand offering him "the finger" and wondered if that *pinche chavolo* hadn't played him for a fool after all.

In the dim lighting, which filtered in through the stained-glass windows, one could just barely make out some of the diablerie which decorated them and the muralled chapel walls. As the gangsters stood there, taking in their surroundings and debating over their next course of action, their discourse was interrupted by the sound of the mission bell ringing a sad, solemn note, its clang reverberating in their bones. As the peal of the first toll still hummed in their ears, there came a second...then a third...there were thirteen in all. It was the ringing of the *diabolus*, calling the wicked to their infernal worship.

Superstitious at heart, the bells set the men on edge; many began to wonder whether they had made a mistake by trying to fight the sorcerer on his own turf. As the last toll dissipated into the eventide darkness, a dirgeful drone was heard to descend from the shadowed rafters of the room, permeating the chapel with phantasmal voices. Abruptly, as if by a thrown switch, the mural walls sprang to life with a growing luminescence as additional candle wicks flared of their own accord with spontaneous flames. Illumined in every recess of the chapel walls lurked the figure of a devil, each with their own name plate. The Seven Princes of Hell they were: Lucifer, Mammon, Asmodeus, Leviathan, Beelzebub, Satan, and Belphegor. In another alcove, locked in a glass cabinet, stood a statue made of some dull black substance which did not reflect the candlelight of the room. Rather the figure absorbed the refulgence, engulfing it in its antithetical substance.

The statue was of a sorcerer in a ceremonial gown and conical cap, looking much like the traditional wizard of fantasy lore. His hands were open in a receptive stance, by his sides, and the expression on his petrified countenance was one of both abject terror and metaphysical ecstasy. The plate at the base of the cabinet read, in Dutch, "A Devotee of Evil"—not that these late-night intruders could tell that, of course. The myriad devils painted on the walls around him seemed almost to taunt him, like Schongauer's Saint Anthony. Revealed as well in the candlelight were the wan spectral countenances of the chorus of revenant monks, whose ghastly faces and funereal tones made the gangsters' hearts sink as they quailed in fear.

Gerardo, a tall thin youth, whipped out a butterfly knife from his pocket and began to recite the *Padre Nuestro* under his breath. Mirruño, meanwhile, ran a quaking hand over his bald pate and swore an oath. Pointing at his eyes, he shouted to his bodyguard, "*Alejo—águila!* Eyes open, man!"

Abruptly, the acrid smell of burnt ozone stung their nostrils, causing them to wince and cough. A black brume whooshed past the men and up to the altar, piercing through everyone present like an icy lance, leaving them all with a fast-spreading numbing chill in their torsos. Gathering at the altar, it swirled into a cone which resembled a tiny tornado, then took on the shape of the black sorcerer, Ba'al Adrian Zwartenberg.

The stunned gangsters froze, rooted to their places, but Mirruño's ire was renewed at the sight of his nemesis. Preparing to lunge, however, he found that his limbs would not obey his will, as if some force was restricting him from acting on his vengeful impulses.

Standing behind the altar was the sorcerer, looking much younger than he did the last time anyone had seen him in public, wearing a cloak covered in black feathers, the lining of which was made of sable silk decorated with esoteric symbols embroidered in gold. The clasp holding it in place about his throat was fashioned from the sooty feet of an Ayam Cemani rooster. Facing the gang before him, he smiled and said, "I know that you've come to kill me. It must have been so hard to gather good intel on my whereabouts when your scouts get their eyes gouged out." At this, the fear-restrained ruffians erupted in a volley of expletives directed towards Zwartenberg.

Holding up his hand and nodding his head in acknowledgment of their ire, he continued, "*However*, I believe the real reason you came here was for my prized poultry, my pet rooster. I heard the plan was to take both the bird and my life. Yes, yes, I know all about it; my faithful servant Diego has already informed me of your scheme to avenge sweet Orfalinda's tarnished honor and subsequent passing. Sorry to hear about that unfortunate turn of events, by the way." His pale lips broke into a smirk as he spoke.

"*¡Canalla!* You don't get to say her name, *brujo*!" shouted Mirruño, straining to free himself from his magical bonds.

"Too late, Lancelot. And you're too late for your revenge plan as well, because I killed the bird myself months ago to retrieve his lone egg—they don't just lay them like hens, you know. Besides, no self-respecting sorcerer would ever keep a rooster in his house. To quote the witch Latoma, from

Montague Summers' treatise on the witchcraft trials of yore, 'That bird is the herald of dawn, he arouses men to the worship of God; and many an odious sin which darkness shrouds will be revealed in the light of day.'"

"Bullshit! Your magic chicken was haunting my Orfalinda just a couple of weeks ago—and then he turned into a cloud and raped her! Diego says you call it *Magistellus*, and that it's a 'familiar' or something. *¡Tu maldita mascota mató a mi querida Orfalinda...mi preciosa Orfalinda!* Your damned pet killed my woman—*pinche gabacho!*"

"Magistellus; a dark cloud, huh? You mean like the one I just materialized from? No, you dunce, I despoiled your ladylove and left a little bit of myself behind, a souvenir of the experience if you will. I am Magistellus! I am the Master!"

As if on cue, the spectral choir renewed their dark chant as Zwartenberg commenced to nigrify and break apart, like a pixelated image, into particles that swirled into a minuscule whirlwind, rearranging into another form, a hybrid form. When the black dust finally settled into place and solidified—a feat which took mere seconds to accomplish—the sorcerer had transmogrified. In place of his smug straw-haired mug, there was a black rooster head of human proportions, with a great black beak and enormous black eyes that looked through one with a startlingly sentient gaze. His nigrous coxcomb quivered as he moved his head in jerky gestures, scanning the small posse which stood planted on the other side of the altar. The long pale hands, which only recently rose from his shirtsleeves, were replaced by sharp black talons.

A shot rang out from the opposite end of the aisle, by the entrance. A lookout, sensing something was amiss, had come to the aid of his comrades, but to no avail. His bullet passed through the black cloud which only moments before had been a solid creature, lodging in the wall behind the altar just above a chryselephantine statue of Eliphas Levi's Baphomet. The swirling particles then swooped down in front of the shooter, tearing out his throat with one swipe of a talon which emerged from within the murk before disappearing again into its mass. As the lookout fell to the ground, choking and bleeding to death, the cloud turned its focus on the remaining men, making short shrift of his mates as they stood helplessly awaiting their respective turn. In a brief and bloody slaughter, they fell, one at a time, as if on an abattoir dis-assembly line. All save for Mirruño, that is.

Stopping to reconstitute in front of the small-time thug, the fiend took physical shape again and cradled the man's bald head in its claws, cocking its own head to stare into his eyes. Soon a voice sounded in Mirruño's head, the voice of the sorcerer, which said, "I laud you, sir, for coming to the defense of your ladylove. Like a true gallant fighting against the unwelcome suitor, the cad, the evil wizard with his dark charms and black magic. Unfortunately, you are no Galahad; you have untold skeletons in your closet, same as I. Your heart is far from pure. Thus, your mojo is weak against my wholly black heart, and your tainted intentions merely led you to my private piece of Hell on Earth. Goodbye for now, and when you see her on the other side, please give Orfalinda a peck on the cheek from me!"

And with that, the were-cock bore its beak into the face of Marcelo "Mirruño" Martinez as his muffled, gurgled cries commingled with the droning of the satanic spectral choir of the Burning Ember Mission of Helldorado.

ZWARTENBERG THE NECROMANCER

For eight nights Ba'al Zwartenberg trafficked amongst the gravestones in the mission boneyard, swathed in the tattered cerements of a Papago man who had been interred in a secluded cairn off-site, though not far enough to escape the purview of the sorcerer and his infernal informants. Once discovered, his harried minion, Diego, dug up the grave, whereupon the warlock leapt into the open cavity and snuggled up to the brittle bones with the familiarity of a lover, after which he took on the habiliments of the ancient cadaver as his own. Now the fearful yet faithful servant would serve the new master of the Burning Ember Mission from his violated grave in the tawny Helldorado brush.

On some nights, the warlock would prowl the Helldorado necropolis and break into the mausoleums of the town elite to take trophies and desecrate their dreamless sleep in a most profane and ungodly manner. On the ninth night, Ba'al Zwartenberg repaired to the mission mortuary chapel with his man Diego to prepare for a Cimmerian ritual: the grim and unholy rite of raising the dead.

The blood-orange moon hung heavy and low like an overripe fruit, fit to burst over the shadow-laden rooftops of the Helldorado eventide. Distant telephone lines and sparse tree branches loomed faintly in the foreground, leaving marly streaks across the ocherous orb, occluding the path of its amber beams. The vesper bell of the Burning Ember Mission clanged, disturbing the resident bats which had taken up in the belfry, causing them to decamp as dirgeful chants issued from within the mission's spectral halls. Carried on rank breezes, this song threaded sinister strands into the windows of neighboring homes and the ears of their quiescent denizens, whispering words of doom and despair to inform their nightmares.

Marching in solemn procession, the Master, clad in the cerements of the grave and fingering the fell charms on his grisly choker, declaimed an insalubrious panegyric, prevailing over the intermittent bleats of a black goat kid that he bore in his arms. At his heels, his ebon-robed acolyte held aloft a ponderous tome: the dreaded *Cultes des Goules* of the Comte d'Erlette. The duo filed into the mission burial vault, wherein awaited an altar draped in a black mantel, surmounted by the accouterments of Thanatotic ritual dimly illumined by inky candles. The atmosphere, redolent with the stench of charnel spoils, was compounded by the burning patchouli emanating from a nearby thurible. In the center of the tomb spread a salt-rimmed circle compassing a vitreous casket with a mummified corpse inside, held in sepulchral quietude. About its neck was strung a jade amulet carven into the likeness of a hound from Hell. The acolyte took up the chant as the supplicant opened the door to the casket, exposing, in all its desiccated splendor, the ghastly occupant therein.

Taking pains not to smudge the circle, he stepped away from the casket. Then, leveling an obsidian athame to the throat of his bleating sacrifice, he drew the blade across, releasing a crimson font which he directed toward a chalice within the circle before stepping back. A murky effluvium soon expelled from the maw of the mummy and wended its way to the chalice, which it temporarily engulfed. Swirling atop the vessel's brim, the tiny whirlwind counter-siphoned the contents of the cup up a pitchy track into the shriveled mouth of the brittle, sallow corpse, which fleshed out with the sanguinary sustenance. Then, with a stertorous gasp and a croak, the revivified revenant shot open its reconstituted eyes and stirred to rise from its narrow house.

Other
Southwestern
Gothic Tales

LUPE SCRIES THE MIRROR BLACK

Lupe scries the mirror black, her purpose to divine

One who'll end her bloody spree, descendent of her line.

Trance begun, her vision starts, she sees her rival clear.

Revelation pierces through her heart just like a spear.

Her sister's only issue, a daughter they call Grace,

Disquieted, but guileless, with an angelic face.

Childless Lupe hoped to drape her niece under crape wings,

And to this novitiate, instill the way of things.

Yet it seems this clever girl, whom she has warmed to know,

Shall mete her retribution, furious with fell blow.

Does she grasp, this hapless child who loves her tía well,

She'll be the one to end her line, and damn herself to Hell?

Are the bodeful images imparted on the glass,

Shadows of unfounded fears, or signs of doom to pass?

For now, Lupe shall abide, to see what will transpire,

And gauge how many nights she's left to leap into the fire.

ALTAGRACIA'S LAMENT

Amidst the Helldorado range, within her cavern lair
Altagracia plays a tune into the midnight air.
Tapping dolorous melodies that echo through the night;
Velvet mallets on an organ, composed of stalagmite.

Woefully wailing her sad keen into the desert night,
As the unbowed scorpion-mouse, squeals in victorious rite.
Night-blooming flowers unfurl buds in welcoming fashion,
Inviting long-nosed bats to lap their sweet nectar with passion.

Ruefully, she pines for the times before the bloodlust came:
The inborn curse which took her aunt, driving Lupe insane.
Forcing her monthly to transform, shedding her human skin
For lupine pelts and raven's wings, imbued by blood and sin.

Altagracia could not bear this curse to carry on,
And so she chose to kill her aunt, nescient of what would come.
By taking the life of Lupe, she hoped more lives to save,
But with the best of intentions the road to Hell is paved.

Tlahuelpuchi cannot be slain by one who shares their line,

The curse just passes to the kin who perpetrate the crime.

By killing Lupe, Grace took on her sanguinary bane,

Along with her occult powers, and transmogrified frame.

A vegetarian at heart, she cannot brook the thirst

For the blood of innocents, with which she has been cursed.

And fight the craving as she might, she cannot shirk her fate,

But rather acquiesce and drink until the thirst abates.

Therefore, she bays unto the moon, coyotes take her cue,

Joining in her lamentation, with guilt and gore imbrued.

Knowing that her isolation will no way stall the curse

From claiming a new-found victim with which to slake her thirst.

Wiping up tears with livid hands, her ululations spent,

She feels the change about to break as she catches a scent.

Her body writhes, her structure pops, the fur begins to spread...

She is now crib-death incarnate, which newborn mothers dread.

DIMAS AKELARRE
THE BRUJO OF NAVARRA

Dimas Akelarre is a swart-hearted man, who plies his craft by night

Worshiping the Black Goat: tributary salute, *osculum infame*

Piping on his *gaita* a lusty saraband, awash in pale moonlight

Misdirecting tyros down a doom-laden route, *itinere flammae*

Like blissful dervishes they whirl across the veil to atramentous realms

Tenanted by creatures: sightless, wan, and grasping; coveting the quick souls.

Careening through hell-fire, on a trail through Sheol, with Dimas at the helm.

Shrieking as they wither, crying when not gasping, upon a track of coals.

Willfully satanic, he walks a darksome path, in fiendish company:

Lucifuge Rofocale and Baphomet round out his coterie.

Misanthropic monsters, intent to undermine and to this world benight.

His fell effluence trills throughout the centuries, tainting wither it flows;

How far its tendrils spread Hell's blight, only the darkness knows.

Féretrina

THERE IS A YOUNG woman whom the Anglos call Coffin-Belly Mary, but that is not her name. Orphaned at an early age, she grew up on the streets of a Mexican border town, where she survived partly by her wits but wasn't hurt by the fact that she was both markedly pretty and possessed of an amiable disposition. These traits made her a favorite of the locals, who freely gave her shelter and alms as they could afford. To make ends meet, she apprenticed with a local *bruja* in return for room and board. Under the tutelage of the sibyl, she learned the trade of a soothsayer: telling fortunes and selling candles, charms, and philters to the lovelorn locals. The *bruja* also introduced her to *La Santa Muerte*, the grim patron saint of the disenfranchised, to whom she became an adherent. When the old woman gave up the ghost, she left her meagre *yerberia* to her protégé, who took to the trade with the aplomb of an adept.

Seemingly favored by Fate, the young woman was also blessed with the good fortune of finding true love at an early age. He was a small-time hood who had a reputation for being tough, but he was always gentle and loving when it came to her. Soon she found herself with child, and they were both so overjoyed at the prospect of bringing a living symbol of their love into the world, they decided that their offspring would have whatever advantages it required to enjoy a better life than they themselves had lived.

The young couple cleaned up their lives, and for the next few months they scrimped and saved, but in a rash last-ditch attempt at making some big money quick to mitigate a move across the border into the US, her young man ran afoul of some malefactors and was never seen again. Devastated by her loss, but determined to give their unborn baby everything she could, she sold the shop, then took what money they had already saved and paid a *coyote* to take her across the border in Nogales, secreted in the back of a hearse.

The trip, though perilous and exhausting, was relatively uneventful, until they reached the other side. Immediately upon their arrival in Arizona, the young woman was sequestered in a shed in the rear of a secluded ranch house where the *coyote* pressured her for more money. When she explained that she had no more to give and no one left in Mexico to get money from, the blackguard did an unthinkable and unforgivable misdeed. He had his henchman hold her arms as he punched the young woman repeatedly in the belly in the hopes she would miscarry, and told her that, once he took care of this *little inconvenience*, he planned to send her to a local maquiladora factory owned by his brother, where she would work until she paid off the rest of the money that he felt she owed him.

As she lay there broken and bloody, alternately drifting in and out of consciousness and weeping in the sweltering heat on the dusty floor of the shed, she cried out to *La Huesuda*, The Bony One, for vengeance on this man, and pleaded with the deity to save her unborn child. She swore that if granted this boon, she would devote the rest of her life to serving *La Santa Muerte*.

Shortly thereafter, in sharp contrast to the scorching temperature outside, the room grew unnaturally cold. The light was sucked out of her surroundings, leaving her in an impenetrable darkness which soon filled with the lamentation of the sorrowful shades of all the lost souls who had perished in that same room, at the hands of this perfidious scoundrel. The wailing grew in pitch and furor until all was stilled by the arrival of the formidable presence of the Lady of the Shadows: *La Huesuda, La Catrina, La Santa Muerte*. She stood there, visible only to the inner eye, in her tenebrous robes and her bony mien, and spoke to the young woman...not with her tongue, which was non-existent, rather with her mind.

"I am Mictecaciuatl, Queen of Mictlan," she said, "and I accept your offer. But the child I cannot save, for he is already here with me, your husband, and my lord, Mictlantecuhtli." And at this she raised her arm to reveal a fleeting glimpse of the wraithlike faces of her beloved family protruding from within the folds of her somber sleeve. "I can, however, give you vengeance upon the men who have perpetrated this great treachery against you. I shall see that they suffer greatly, and their souls will be enthralled to you, effectuating your bidding throughout eternity. Though in life they took the byname of coyotes, in death they shall instead wear the skin of the Xoloitzcuintle who, like their namesake the psychopomp Xolotl, guide souls of the newly dead on their journey to Mictlan. They shall herald your arrival with their howls and protect you from your enemies.

"You shall remain indefinitely as you are today, young and fair, although a child-woman you shall no longer be, for you shall be an emissary of the Queen of Mictlan, and no one shall dare excise the unborn babe from your belly, for it shall become a conduit through which I may communicate with my people in the world of the living. The tiny bones in your belly shall become a portal key through which the soul of your unborn son shall periodically enter to relay messages and directives from me in the Underworld. You shall find a black blade buried in the brow of the wretch who took your son from you: retrieve it, and cut a bone from him. It shall become a powerful talisman, which will serve as a warning to those who would do you harm. Take the hides of the *coyotes* as well, and wear them, for they shall give you power over their subservient souls and strike fear into the heart of your enemies."

"But where can I go that people will not become suspicious of a foreigner who does not speak their language, does not age, and carries a child that never comes to term?" the young woman asked.

"Do not fret, Mother of Sorrow. You shall not have to bear the weight of a swollen belly for eternity, but when I must speak to you, you shall feel your son's bones rattle in your belly. If you have a query for me, touch your abdomen and think upon your son, and his spirit will fly from Mictlan to the bones inside you to hear his mother's voice and come to her aid. Moreover, I have followers in many places who will gladly give you shelter; once they see your gift, they will know you speak for me. They shall call you Féretrina, after *féretro*, the Spanish word for coffin, because you shall carry the bones of your unborn son within you as a reliquary wherever you go. As for language barriers, there will be none. You shall understand all who speak to you and they shall understand you. Do I not address you now in the speech of my people's conquerors? Nay, fear not, no foreign tongue shall keep you from communicating my message to the ones who would hear it.

"When you leave this small house of your heartbreak, go to the lair of your despoiler and you shall find him dead. Enter freely and without fear. Draw a bath to cleanse yourself of the dross of your suffering and what remains of your former life. Fortify yourself with food from his larder, then rest, for you soon shall embark on a quest in my name to come to the aid of my adherents and devotees in their own times of need."

And so, the young woman accepted the divine will of the Queen of Mictlan, whilst the dark lady opened her robe again to accept the desolate souls cowering in the coldest corners of the room before returning to her shadowy realm. As the light slowly returned along with the heat, the young woman sat up and looked around to see the blood that lately covered herself and the floor was gone, most likely taken by the goddess upon her withdrawal. Once she gathered her senses, she stood up and tried the door. Finding it unlocked, she staggered into the daylight.

Wincing from the harsh brightness, the first thing she focused on was a black walnut tree, a *nogal cimarrón*, the namesake of the twin border towns which bore the route of pain and sorrow she had traveled to find her new life. She contemplated the great black-barked tree, with its sprawling gnarled branches reaching out into the dust-heavy firmament, and marveled how its fleshy green fruit bore such a hard and blackened seed within its core, much like the macabre treasure within her abdomen.

Now, accustomed to the glare of unrelenting sunlight, she walked up to the ranch house and found the door open, so she trod over the threshold without fear, as she had been instructed to by Mictecacihuatl. Upon entering the house, she found the flayed bodies of three men, the two who had held and beaten her and taken the life of her unborn son as well as another man, presumably the aforesaid brother. Their severed heads had been placed on wooden staves torn from an outdoor fence, which were driven deep into their respective torsos; the sightless, lidless eyes of their twisted and harrowed faces bulged in expressions of horror and pain, which brought a mirthless smile to her lips.

Spying a darkly glittering object protruding from the forehead of one of the men, she approached it to find that it was a ceremonial knife made from obsidian, a black volcanic glass used much by the ancient Aztec peoples in their jewelry, ceremonial implements, and weapons. She took the knife from the dead man's brow and proceeded to cut the tibia bone from his leg, which she placed in a coffret she found set in front of the gory remains that contained the tanned hides of the three rogues. Setting the box aside, she sought out the bathroom to wash away the sweat and filth from her body, after which she changed her clothes, then rifled through the cupboards in the kitchen for something to eat and settled on a comforting cup of champurrado.

At nightfall, she heard the howls of her canine retinue keening outside the house. Opening the door, she let them in to feast on the carcasses of their past wicked incarnations; then, leaving her remaining worldly possessions behind, she picked up the coffret containing her gruesome trophies, stepped out the front door and into the night, walking northward toward her destiny. As *Mictecacihuatl* had promised, wherever she went she found shelter and succor with devotees of *La Santa Muerte*, who knew her by her Xolo companions, her black cassock and like-colored cope fashioned from some curious hides, tanned and embroidered beautifully in gold by an acolyte, and the ear spools she wore, hewn from the leg bone of the wretch who sealed the fate of her unborn baby boy. The boy she now called *Nogalito*, her little black walnut.

Gramercy

I would like to thank the people who helped me finally unleash this story into the world at large. For starters, thanks to my friend Patricia Lynn Dompieri, whose challenge inspired me to write this dark tale in the first place. I would also like to thank my friend, fellow author/poet Scott J. Couturier, whose editing suggestions helped me prune back the deadwood and fellow Weird Poet Society member Frank Coffman for his helpful suggestions on "Dimas Akelarre."

I would like to thank authors Rebecca Buchanan, Hayley Arrington, and Suzy Jacobson Cherry for their input, especially on the scenes concerning the characterization of Orfalinda, as well as Jay Sandoval for his suggestions on how a feisty Latina might rebuff an unwelcome suitor in Spanish. Ms. Buchanan was also kind enough to take a look at "Féretrina" for me and had some very kind words to say about it, which helped cinch my decision to include it in this collection.

I would like to thank my friend, artist Dick Kelly, for agreeing to take a shot at the artwork, even if I ended up choosing a different route, and I thank Mutartis Boswell for taking up the mantle, so to speak, on such short notice. His incredible artwork has really brought my dark vision to life. I would also like to thank my friend Peter Kulikowski for recording my recitation of excerpts from this collection, and for his other assistance.

Lastly, I would like to thank my friend, editor/illustrator/publisher Dan Sauer, the driving force behind Jackanapes Press, for taking this on last minute, despite having a full roster of releases on his plate. I know my pet project will be in good hands.

About the Author

MANUEL ARENAS IS A writer of verse and prose in the Gothic Horror tradition. His work has appeared in *Spectral Realms* and *Penumbra*, both from Hippocampus Press, and in sundry genre anthologies. He has recently released his first collection of prose and poetry, *Book of Shadows: Grim Tales and Gothic Fancies*, from Jackanapes Press, and is currently working on a follow-up volume. He resides in Phoenix, Arizona, where he pens his dark ditties sheltered behind heavy curtains, shunning the oppressive orb which glares down on him from the cloudless, dust-filled sky.

About the Artist

MUTARTIS BOSWELL IS AN English artist hailing from the rural West of the UK, where he lives with his partner and two kids while creating his weird and atmospheric worlds. He's worked as an artist for Feral House and Dynatox Ministries, and his illustrations have appeared in various weird fiction publications such as *Spectral Realms*, *Occult Detective Magazine*, and many others. He also makes underground comix and has been a regular contributor to Satanic Mojo Comix and Dystopian Chronicles. More of his art can be seen at boswellart.blogspot.com and boswellart.bigcartel.com.

Paul 'Mutartis' Boswell

Weird and Wonderful,
illustration, concept work,
screenprinting, mural painting.
pboswell66@gmail.com
boswellart.bigcartel.com

ShadowScapes
PRESENTS

A SELECTION OF READINGS FROM
THE BURNING EMBER MISSION OF HELLDORADO
BY MANUEL ARENAS

Read by the author and accompanied by suitably atmospheric music and effects.

Available to stream or download at BandCamp via the URL or QR code below:

https://shadowscapes.bandcamp.com/album/the-burning-ember-mission